2/13/8

Dear Baby

✝✝✝✝✝✝✝✝✝✝

Dear Baby

✦✦✦✦✦✦✦✦✦✦✦✦✦✦✦✦✦

Joanne Rocklin

Illustrated by
Eileen McKeating

Macmillan Publishing Company   New York

Collier Macmillan Publishers   London

Macmillan Publishing Company
866 Third Avenue, New York, NY 10022
Collier Macmillan Canada, Inc.
First Edition
Printed in the United States of America

10 9 8 7 6 5 4 3 2 1

The text of this book is set in 13 point Bembo.
The illustrations are rendered in pencil.

Library of Congress Cataloging-in-Publication Data
Rocklin, Joanne.
Dear baby / Joanne Rocklin: illustrated by Eileen McKeating.—
1st ed.   p.   cm.
Summary: During the months that her mother is expecting, eleven-
year-old Farla writes a series of letters to the unborn baby
describing her feelings toward family members, friends, and her
future brother or sister.
ISBN 0-02-777320-5
[1. Family life—Fiction.   2. Babies—Fiction.   3. Letters.]
I. McKeating, Eileen, ill.   II. Title.
PZ7.B59De   1988   [Fic]—dc19
87-36468   CIP   AC

For

Michael and Eric

✦✦✦✦✦✦✦✦✦✦

✦✦✦✦✦✦✦✦✦✦ Wednesday, October 4

Dear Baby,

You will be born in about six months. You will be my new brother or my new sister, I don't know which yet. My name is Farla.

If you could talk, you would probably say, "Hey, Farla, I'm just minding my own business, waiting to be born. I can't read your letter. I can't write you back. Why are you writing to me?"

Good question, baby, very good question. According to the book Mom bought me called *The Wondrous Story: From Zygote to Baby,* you are only three teensy inches long. You weigh one ounce. All you do is float around inside Mom, back and forth, back and forth, doing absolutely nothing of any importance. Except change my entire life, that's all. One little old ounce, and you can do that.

But here I am, writing to you. It was Mom's idea and my sixth-grade teacher Ms. Roseman-Keller's. Mom's a graduate student in psychology, and she says that ever since she married Charlie last year and Great-aunt Sally came to help out around here and I started twitching my left eye like I used to in kindergarten, she knew I wasn't coping well with my feelings. Ms.

Roseman-Keller says I've been making careless mistakes in math and I'm not working up to my potential. So Mom and Ms. Roseman-Keller and I had an after-school conference to get me to express my feelings. And I did. That was the easy part.

I said I was mad. I said I thought Charlie was okay and that I was glad Mom was having so much fun with him, but I never thought it was going to mean we had to live with him every day of our lives! I told them we didn't really need Great-aunt Sally helping around the house. (Actually she's Charlie's great-aunt, who acts like she's my grandmother or something. She knows I have a perfectly wonderful grandmother who lives in Brooklyn, New York.)

And I said I was sad, too. I was thinking about my dad a lot. He got cancer when I was seven years old, and died. Telling my feelings was easy. Feeling better about everything was the hard part.

Then Mom said, "And the baby makes everything final, doesn't it, honey?"

I just nodded and felt that big gurgly lump in my throat that only gets bigger when I try not to cry. I didn't want to cry in front of a teacher, especially Ms. Roseman-Keller. She expects a lot of maturity from her sixth-graders

because she's preparing us for junior high. "It's no use," I said. "I've expressed every single one of my feelings, and I still feel bad." Then Ms. Roseman-Keller said to Mom, "Farla has a special talent for writing. Maybe you can think of a way she could use that talent to help her feel better."

That compliment made me feel good even though I didn't really understand what she was talking about. I like to write stories about danger and love and desert islands and turbulent seas. Ms. Roseman-Keller says I have a vivid imagination. But my feelings are *real*. I wish you weren't coming, unborn baby, and that's not a story I'm making up!

After I went to bed that night, hugging my gray cat, Treat, under the blankets, I could hear everybody talking about me.

MOM: (Mumble, mumble) so sensitive (mumble)
CHARLIE: When I (mumble) help her (mumble)
GREAT-AUNT SALLY: Young people today (mumble, mumble) the baby

The next day Mom gave me a present. It was one of those books with a beautiful artistic cover (fuchsia roses, my favorite flower and my favorite color) and white clean empty pages inside.

4

The kind of book that is so beautiful, you never want to cross out or even erase. The kind of book you are supposed to write beautiful, wise, and special thoughts in.

Mom said, "Why don't you write some letters to this new unborn baby? Tell the baby the story about what life was like for you before it came into our world. Then you can read what you write to the baby when he or she gets older, if you want to."

So here I am, writing to you, unborn baby, writing in the book with the beautiful artistic cover. But my thoughts are not beautiful. My thoughts are sad and worried. And the more I write, the more I realize what I have to do.

You see, unborn baby, I have a plan in mind.

Farla

✦✦✦✦✦✦✦✦✦✦ Thursday, October 12

Dear Baby,

I bet you're wondering (if an unborn baby can wonder) what my plan is. I've been thinking about it a lot. I will be moving to Brooklyn to live with my grandmother. There. I never said those words out loud even to myself (which I just did, just now). I think it's a very good plan. I will be moving to Brooklyn to live with my grandmother. I shall be departing for Brooklyn to reside with my late father's mother. I plan to pull up stakes for Brooklyn to abide with Bubbie Flo. Any way you say it, it's a good idea.

Bubbie Flo doesn't know it yet, but I'm sure she'll think it's a good idea, too. She misses me as much as I miss her. I am her only grandchild. My dad was her only son. We are true flesh-and-blood kin through and through. We even look alike. We both have noses that are round and sort of look like mushrooms. We both have brown eyes. (So did my dad.) She says her hair was reddish brown like mine before it got gray. She loves cats, like I do, and takes in strays. We both love potato pancakes more than almost any other food. I visit her every winter vacation, and she makes piles and piles of potato pancakes, called *latkes,* for Hanukkah. She grates the potatoes by hand until her fingers get scraped, but she says she does it with love in her heart. Her kitchen smells like good food, and she smells and feels like a fat clean pillow.

Mom will be busy with you, and busy being

a wife and all that. She'll miss me and I'll miss her, but nothing will be the same when you come. Nothing's the same even now, and you're just a round bulge in her tummy.

First of all, Mom's a student. She does homework and studies. She used to be a secretary. She would come home at five-thirty and kick off her high heels and say, "Boy, I'm pooped! Let's go grab a pizza!" (Or some *moo-shu* or some tacos or some hamburgers and fries.) She used to watch TV with me, and we'd make popcorn together and bake cookies. Sometimes we'd even go to the movies on a school night after I did *my* homework. We can't do that anymore because of all *her* homework.

She's a wife now, too. She's Charlie's wife. Your father, not mine. She used to be a wife to my father and then a single parent to me. So now she's a wife again, which means she talks to her husband a lot. They discuss things like the President and taxes and bills and people I don't know. She giggles all the time. She thinks Charlie's jokes are funnier than I do.

SAMPLE JOKE:
Knock, knock!
Who's there?

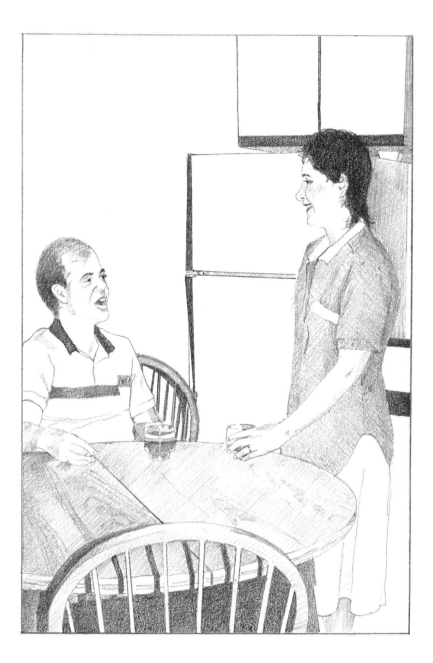

Transylvania Times! Get it?

No.

Neither do I. I get the *L.A. Times.*

Har-dee-har-har. And of course, being a wife means that you sleep in this gigantic king-size bed with your husband. She used to have a much smaller bed, which was just big enough for her (and me if I ever had a bad dream or something and needed to crawl in with her. Naturally that's out of the question now, not that I'd even want to anymore.) I don't understand why they need such a big bed. It's like a trampoline. And Charlie snores.

Your dad's nice, don't get me wrong. That's part of the trouble. He's too nice. It makes me feel mixed up and guilty to be mad at someone who is nice. I'm trying very hard to understand it, so I made a list of things that bug me about him.

1. He acts as if he lives here. Which he does. But Mom and I were living at 404 Elmby Avenue first.
2. He's four years younger than Mom. She's thirty-six and he's thirty-two, but they look okay together. Mom is short and cute and he's got a bald spot, so the age difference sort of evens out. But when

9

she was in the sixth grade like me, he
was in the second grade reading stories
about little bears and talking trains and
stuff. That's weird.
3. He takes too many pictures. He works
   for an insurance company, but photography is his hobby. Every time I turn
   around, he's taking candid pictures, and
   I don't like the way my nose turns out
   in pictures, but I don't want anyone to
   know that.
4. He's Protestant. We're Jewish. There's
   nothing wrong with that, I guess. It just
   feels different.
5. He has a book called *How to Be a Better
   Stepparent* on his night table. And once
   he was reading a big red book in the den,
   and when I came in, he said, "Hi, kid!"
   and blushed almost as red as the book.
   Then he closed it with a bookmark
   and turned on the news. Later I snuck
   into Mom and Charlie's room and
   opened the red book to where the bookmark was. I'm not really a sneaky person, but I couldn't help myself. I actually
   thought it was going to be about sex.
   But it wasn't. The book was called *From
   Tot to Teen*. I copied the underlined parts:

Twelve is learning how to socialize and often has a well-developed sense of humor. S/he is becoming aware of grooming and physical appearance and shows some budding interest in the opposite sex. Twelve can be enthusiastic about and challenged by school. Emotions vacillate between highs and lows, and Twelve is often self-critical. Twelve's outward affection toward parents may not be as prevalent as Eleven's.

I am *his* homework. (I will be twelve years old in May.) I feel like a fly specimen. Phooey.

6. He is related to Great-aunt Sally. More about her later.

7. And here is what makes me feel worst of all: His eyes are blue. That sounds crazy, I know. Why do I feel sad about that, you would ask if you could, unborn baby.

I will answer when I write again. Treat has just come upstairs to tell me that it's our bedtime. I'm sleepy.

Farla

P.S. I'm keeping my plan to move to Brooklyn a secret because I'm going to surprise Bubbie Flo. She's a very generous-hearted person. Every time somebody comes to visit her, she cooks and cooks and cooks, and if she knew that I was planning on moving there, she'd probably take out part of her life's savings from the bank to fix up her back room just for me and buy me new school clothes, etc. I want to be as little trouble as possible, so I'll tell her about my plans when I go there in December. "We're family!" I'll say.

✦✦✦✦✦✦✦✦✦✦✦✦ Friday, October 20

Dear Baby,

I was just looking at your picture in *The Wondrous Story: From Zygote to Baby*. Of course, it's not a picture of the real you, but how you probably look right now inside Mom at over three months old. You look like a drowned guinea pig, in my opinion. The book says you are starting to grow bones around this time. You can open and close your mouth. You get nourishment from a long cord inside Mom, called her umbilical cord, which is attached to your belly button. This would all be very interesting if it were someone else's mom's umbilical cord they were talking about.

Like I said before, nobody knows yet whether you are a boy or a girl. But *I* know something about you for sure, and it makes me feel lousy. Remember Charlie's blue eyes that were upsetting me? (I mentioned them in my last letter to you.) Well, unborn baby, you've got them, too.

The reason I know is that Ms. Roseman-Keller is teaching us a little bit about genetics. Ms. Roseman-Keller is the kind of teacher who teaches stuff because it's fascinating and not just because it's required. She says she wants to expand our minds and sharpen our curiosity. So we know about some Greek philosophers and what photosynthesis is and we've read a bit of Shakespeare. We know all about the solar system and how the computer was invented. And we know about genetics.

Ms. Roseman-Keller says that each trait we have—our hair, our eyes, how tall we are, etc.—comes from two genes. One gene is from the mother and one gene is from the father. Some genes are stronger, or more dominant, than other genes. Brown-eye genes are more dominant than genes for other colors, so if you get a brown-eye gene from one parent and a blue-eye gene from the other, for example, you end up with brown eyes. That's how I got my brown eyes, because my dad had brown eyes and my mom has blue eyes.

Or you could get a weaker gene from each parent, called a recessive gene, and that's how you'd get light-colored eyes. By the way, brown-eyed parents can have a blue-eyed kid if they both have hidden blue-eye genes that they both give to their kid. But blue-eyed parents can't have brown-eyed kids because they have no dominant brown-eye genes to pass along. So therefore:

$$\begin{array}{r} \text{MOM'S BLUE EYES} \\ + \text{ CHARLIE'S BLUE EYES} \\ \hline = \text{UNBORN BABY'S BLUE EYES} \end{array}$$

Minus Farla's brown eyes. I'm not going to be around to feel like the odd man out. Nosiree. You guys can hang around Los Angeles staring at each other with your big blue eyes, but I'm off to brown-eyed Bubbie Flo's, where I know I'll fit in.

About that nourishment you're getting. If you're finding it pretty boring, it's because it's from Great-aunt Sally's boring cooking. She makes well-balanced meals based on the Basic Food Groups. She cooks piles more vegetables than Mom ever did. If I refuse to eat any of them, like brussels sprouts, for instance, she asks, "How do you know you won't like it if you won't even taste it?" But I do know, I always say, by the way it *looks.* Especially brussels sprouts, so bald and creepy-looking. And we hardly ever go out for pizza or hamburgers or tacos or *moo-shu* like Mom and I used to practically every single week. Mom has to drink lots and lots of milk because of your bones, unborn baby. I don't know what *your* bones have to do with *my* bones, but all of a sudden I have to drink three entire glasses of milk a day. And Great-aunt Sally keeps track.

Great-aunt Sally is a retired teacher. She used to live in San Diego, but Mom and Charlie asked her to move to L.A. to be nearer to her new family. They said she could live with us until she gets settled. Great-aunt Sally says the least she can do is cook and help with the cleaning until you come along. A person could go blind from the shine around here. Mom's motto is "Clean enough to be healthy, dirty enough to be happy." I think that's a pretty good motto. But Great-aunt Sally has a different one. Hers is

"Cleanliness is next to godliness." So now when I come home from school, almost the first words I hear are, "Wipe your feet, dear. I just vacuumed."

When she's not cleaning, she spends her time knitting things for you. Silly-looking sweaters with holes in them and little hats with lots of ribbons and pom-poms.

I bet she was a very strict teacher. Not like Ms. Roseman-Keller, who is kind and cheerful (even though she expects us to do our very best work) and who has beautiful long curly hair and wears stockings with tiny stars or butterflies on them. Charlie says that all the young men were in love with Great-aunt Sally and *her* long beautiful hair "in her day." I find that extremely hard to believe. Now she wears her hair in a tight black knot on the back of her head. And I happen to know that her knot of hair, which has lots of hairpins stuck in it, comes off at night.

I am writing this letter in bed. I can hear the sound of knitting needles and Charlie's snoring. I can smell Mom's cologne, Whiff o' Roses, because she came into my room to kiss me goodnight. But mostly I smell Window Sparkle and Bathroom Pride. It doesn't smell or feel like the same old house at all.

Farla

✝✝✝✝✝✝✝✝✝✝✝✝ Friday, October 27

Dear Baby,

You probably think (if an unborn baby can think) that I'm a great big grouch. I wasn't always like this, just since all these changes (including you) started happening.

GRR—OUCH. Grouch is a very good word. Some words sound the way they mean, and this is one of them. When I'm a grouch, I am angry (GRR!) and sad and hurting (OUCH!) at the same time. But sometimes I can also feel happy for no reason at all, then blue a little later. I sort of feel like the silver mercury in a very busy thermometer. Mom says when you are entering adolescence, this is normal.

Today I am happy for a reason. I made a new friend at school. Actually Ms. Roseman-Keller assigned her to me. (Ms. Roseman-Keller always assigns "buddies" to new people to show them around the school.) Her name is Lorraine, and she is from Toronto, Canada. A lot of other kids in the class wanted to be Lorraine's buddy, especially because she comes from a foreign land. Roy, a boy in my class who really should be in kindergarten because he is very immature for his age, went up to Lorraine and said, "Chevrolet coupay see voo play?" and Lorraine replied very

sweetly and politely, more politely than Roy deserved, that she was not French, that the city of Toronto was in the province of Ontario, which wasn't the French-speaking part of Canada. This was new information to me, too.

Lorraine is a special person, even if she doesn't speak French. She is very elegant, I think. She wears pearl earrings. She has a soft voice and small feet and a nose that turns up. (My feet are growing much faster than the rest of me, my nose is round, and I wish my voice were quiet and soft like hers. I yell a lot. I got into the habit from shouting up and down the stairs at home.)

So I showed Lorraine the principal's office and the nurse's office and the girls' bathrooms. We had a lot of things to talk about. I told her I was born in Los Angeles and that my mother used to be a widow, but she got married again and was going to have a baby. She told me that her parents have been married for *twenty years!* Her father's business transferred them here. She has two older sisters, Marlene, who is in high school, and Cheryl, who is in college and sometimes is a model in Sears catalogs. Lorraine's favorite food is chocolate truffles, and she has a canary named Soprano. She has a very large vocabulary because her hobby is collecting words. She tries to use one new word a day in her actual conversations. But she says that she is terrible in math.

"Here's an idea," I said, trying to make my voice sound soft and elegant like hers, "I can help you with your math, and maybe you can help me expand my vocabulary."

"Sure," she said. "This is what I do. Each morning I open my dictionary to any page at all, close my eyes, and let my finger run down the page, counting to five. The word it stops at is my word for the day!"

"That's a great technique!" I said.

"No, it's a superlative one! *Superlative* is my word for the day!"

Lorraine said she didn't mind if I copied her dictionary technique. Then we decided to use our own words for the day in our future conversations with each other, and that way we could learn each other's words, too.

After school, walking home, we discovered that we lived around the corner from each other! Lorraine lives in the big house right next door to the Haunted House.

The Haunted House has had this FOR SALE sign on its front lawn for years and years. No one wants to buy it. It is very big, and you can tell that it was once a beautiful house. But now the windows and doors are boarded up, the paint is peeling, and the grass is long and wild. A big ugly palm tree guards the front lawn. Everybody has always called it the Haunted House because it looks so creepy. When I was little, I used to ride by on my tricycle, pedaling fast, looking straight ahead so I wouldn't have to see it. Now I like to make up stories about it.

I don't understand why it happened, but all of a sudden I started telling Lorraine a story about the Haunted House, making it up right then and there and telling it to her like I really believed it was true. I told her that a long time ago an actor had lived there, but that he had been murdered under mysterious circumstances. I told her that some people say he still roams around inside, shouting lines from old movies and TV commercials.

"Oh, come on, Farla," said Lorraine. "That's not true!"

"Well, that's the scoop around Hollywood." Then my imagination went crazy. "See that little window on the second floor?" I said. "That's the actor's daughter's room. The handsome actor had it painted fuchsia because it was his daughter's favorite color. But a tragedy occurred. One day, after a hard day acting in the movies, the actor was writing a letter to his beloved wife, who was an opera singer and who had traveled to Italy with their daughter to perform. Two thugs climbed in the kitchen window and hit him over the head with a silver candlestick. The mother and daughter remained in Italy to sing sad songs forever, and the actor still haunts the house."

"That's a superlative story! You have a good imagination," said Lorraine.

I can't believe what I shouted at her as she walked toward her house. "Even the swimming pool is haunted! Once I was walking by the house, and I heard splashing noises coming from the backyard, and the pool was empty!"

Sometimes I think I have water on the brain. Lorraine must think I'm nuts.

Farla

✦✦✦✦✦✦✦✦✦✦✦Sunday, November 5

Dear Baby,

I have to hand it to you. According to *The Wondrous Story,* you have quadrupled your weight and doubled your length in the past month. You now weigh four ounces and are over six inches long. If I quadrupled my weight and doubled my height, I'd now weigh three hundred pounds and be nine feet tall.

Mom says she can feel you moving around inside of her, like a tiny butterfly winging its way. The doctor can hear your heart beating, with a stethoscope. This week Mom is going to have a special test. She says the doctor takes a little bit of the fluid that you are floating around in, grows a culture with it like in a science experiment, and then examines the cells under a microscope in a few weeks. By doing all that, they can tell if you are going to develop normally. They can even tell if you are going to be a boy or a girl.

Ms. Roseman-Keller told us that a long time ago a wise French philosopher named Descartes said, "I think, therefore I am." I wonder if Descartes ever switched that sentence around and said, "I am, therefore I think." Can you think, unborn baby? Are you dreaming while you sleep? What can you dream about except the feeling of warmness and the sound of water and faraway voices?

I wish I were growing up as fast as you are. I counted forty-five girls in the sixth grade who are starting to develop. Breasts, that is. I myself haven't started to develop yet. My only consolation is that my new friend, Lorraine, hasn't started, either. But she still looks and acts more sophisticated than I do. She knows things, like what you say to your boyfriend and how to dance and how to order French food in restaurants. She says she learns a lot of things from her two older sisters, Cheryl and Marlene.

I realized I had a lot of developing to do on the night of Halloween. I had invited Lorraine to go trick-or-treating with me, since she was new in the neighborhood and I would be able to take her to the most generous neighbors for candy. We had decided to dress up as ghost twins. We planned to cut out black-paper chains for around our ankles and smear black mascara around our eyes. The rest of the costume would be the usual old white sheet with eyes cut out.

On Halloween Eve I couldn't wait to put on my ghost costume. I found my plastic pumpkin candy basket in the garage. Mom let me use her black mascara, and I made my eyes big and spooky. When Charlie saw me, he fell down on the floor, pretending to faint from fear. Of course, Mom thought that was pretty hilarious.

But when Lorraine answered her door, she wasn't wearing her ghost costume, the twin to mine.

"I'm really sorry, Farla," she said. "I should have called you. You see, I went upstairs to put on my costume. I had the sheet and the chains all ready, but I just couldn't put them on."

"But why not?" I asked. "Didn't your costume fit you?"

"It's not that," she said. "I couldn't put it on because I remembered that Marlene and Cheryl stopped trick-or-treating way before they were twelve. I think that trick-or-treating is to be part of my childish past."

I suddenly felt very silly in my sheet with some old paper wrapped around my ankle. I could feel my cheeks getting red, even though you couldn't see that under my sheet. It was humiliating.

"I was feeling a bit too old for this myself," I said, lying. "I was really doing it for my neighbors, who get a kick out of seeing me all dressed up."

"We can still have a superlative time," said Lorraine.

And we did. We made popcorn and watched movies on her VCR. The doorbell rang and rang all night, and we were the big kids giving out candies to all the little kids.

Lorraine was right. At almost-twelve it was time to make trick-or-treating a part of my childish past. I only wish I had realized that on my own.

Farla

✝✝✝✝✝✝✝✝✝✝✝ Friday, November 10

Dear Madeleine, Veronica, Annabelle,
Eric, Lee, Edward, or Daniel,
   Those are the names Mom and Charlie have been talking about for you. They have a book called *5000 Names for Your Baby,* which they look at a lot.
   I looked up Farla in that book, but even though there were 5000 names, Farla was no-where to be found. Mom said she was watching an old movie late at night when she was big and fat and pregnant with me and she couldn't fall asleep. Farla was the name of the heroine's funny best friend. Mom said she laughed so hard during the movie, she had her best night's sleep in weeks. So she decided to name me Farla after that funny friend.
   I found Mom's name, Amanda, in the name

book. It means "lovable." The book also gives the *var.* and *dim.* of the name. *Var.* means "variant." That's a different way of spelling the name. *Dim.* stands for "diminutive," how you would make the name cuter, like a nickname. The *dims.* for Amanda are Manda and Mandy. Charlie and Chuck are the *dims.* for Charles, which means "man." My father's name was Sampson, or Sam for short. Sampson means "solar," or "the sun's man." Lorraine means "famous in battle," and the *var.* and *dim.* are Laraine and Lori. Lorraine says her name fits her perfectly because she plans to use her talent for words to become a famous lawyer who always wins her battles in the courtroom.

I've always wanted a nickname. A nickname makes you feel special. I think if Mom had put a little bit of thought into it, she could have come up with a name for me with a meaning, a *var.*, and a *dim.* What can you make out of Farla? Far-Far? La-La?

Farla

Dear Baby,

I wasn't going to tell you how your parents met, but I guess you have a right to know. It's not a very romantic story. They advertised for each other. Each of them put an ad in this special magazine for single adults, describing themselves and describing what they desired in the perfect mate. Mom said she wanted to meet a man who was steady and kind and liked Mozart and communicating. Charlie said he wanted to meet someone who was attractive and gentle, who liked to converse, and who enjoyed photography. They both answered each other's ad. Mom and Charlie say they got exactly what they wanted, and more. Mom isn't really a photographer herself, but she says she's an admirer of Charlie's pictures, and he says that's all right with him. He says he doesn't like Mozart as much as Mom does, but more than he thought he would. Mom says she's surprised at how funny Charlie turned out to be, since he was so serious and formal on their first date. Charlie says he's surprised and glad she thinks he's so funny. I say, he should be.

SAMPLE JOKE:
QUESTION: What do you call a bunch of

bunnies hopping backward?
ANSWER: A receding hare line.

Har-dee-har-har.

Mom and my real dad met when she was a waitress and he was a cook in an Italian restaurant. They were both working their way through college. Sometimes I lie in bed at night, imagining how they fell in love:

YOUNG MAN: Amanda, would you please taste this marinara sauce—Why, your eyes! I've never noticed that they were so aquamarine!

YOUNG WOMAN: You flatter me, Sampson. May I have my order, please?

Their fingers touch as he hands her the plate of spaghetti. An electric current runs through their bodies as her aquamarine eyes and his brown eyes meet. They know at that very moment that they are meant to be married and have one child, a daughter, the symbol of their great undying love.

THE BEGINNING

I wish my dad were still alive, and he and Mom could have been married for years and years like Lorraine's parents. I can still remember how he smelled like the wind and the rain on flowers and how tall he was. I am looking at a picture of him right now. In the picture a three-year-old me is sitting on his shoulders, and we are both laughing.

I can hear Mom and Charlie laughing downstairs. It has not been a good evening. Here is what happened:

After dinner Mom and Charlie and Great-aunt Sally went into the den, where Mom always studies, Charlie listens to classical music, and Great-aunt Sally knits. Mom called me into the den. She and Charlie were both smiling and staring down at something spread out on the coffee table.

"Look at what Charlie's done, Farla. Aren't they great?" Mom asked.

"They" were three black-and-white photographs: a picture of a shiny apple framed in red, a picture of a plump bear cub framed in blue, and a picture of a sports car framed in yellow.

"Nice pictures, Charlie," I said. I didn't know what else to say. His photographs were usually much more interesting. These were kind of, well, simple.

"A is for?" asked Charlie.

"Apple," said Mom.

"B is for?"

"Bear," said Mom.

"And C is for?"

"Car!" said Mom. Then they both looked at me with goofy, happy smiles on their faces.

"So?" I asked.

"These are alphabet pictures for the baby's room," said Mom.

"We're going to give the baby your little room, and I'm going to convert the spare room downstairs into a nice bedroom just for you, with built-in bookshelves," said Charlie.

"Oh, that's okay, Charlie," I said. "Thanks, anyway. I think I'll stay in the room upstairs. I like my window seat."

"Honey, that's a decision that's already been made," Mom said. "It's warmer upstairs, and I want the baby to be near me for nighttime feedings. And, anyway, now you'll have a nice big room for sleep-overs with your friends."

Just like that. No discussion at all. I love my little room! It has a wonderful window seat for dreaming and reading, just the right size for Treat and me.

Then Treat herself strolled into the room and headed for Great-aunt Sally's yarn. Mom picked her up, and she snuggled into Mom's lap.

"That cat sheds an enormous amount of

hair," said Great-aunt Sally. "She sure increases my vacuuming."

Mom frowned. "Treat's not a kitten any longer. I think she should be spending her time outdoors. Cat hair and babies just don't mix."

Treat purred, as if she were thanking Mom for a compliment. She didn't realize that her days indoors were numbered. I felt so bad for her. I excused myself and said I wanted to listen to my own kind of music—rock—upstairs in my room.

Mom thinks everything's okay because I'm getting my feelings out, writing all these letters to you, unborn baby. I'm writing down my angry feelings, but they're not going away. *I'm* going away. To Brooklyn. They can rent out that cold converted spare room to a boarder for all I care.

Farla

✦✦✦✦✦✦✦✦✦✦✦ Friday, November 17

Dear Baby,

For the past few days, Treat has been an outdoor cat, on Mom's orders. We put her litter box outside, as well as her red food bowl and her water dish.

Yesterday Lorraine came over after school, and we did our homework in the backyard while we watched Treat getting used to the great outdoors. Lorraine had brought her canary, Soprano, in its cage. She had brought her canary for two reasons:

1. To give it a taste of being around trees and nature like its ancient canary ancestors, in order to improve its singing.
2. To train Treat to be kind to birds and other small animals, and not be a predator.

Treat pranced around the yard, sniffing and scratching and staring. Every time she snooped around Soprano's cage, we both yelled, "No, Treat, no!" But that didn't do any good, so we had to hang the cage on a tree branch.

I like Lorraine a lot. She is so kind. Even though I am her teacher-appointed buddy, she says we were meant to be friends. For instance, we have the same favorite books, we listen to the same radio station, and we both have a tiny mole in the same place on the inside of our left ankle. Lorraine says I am helping to ease the pain she feels because she had to leave her good friend Doreen in Toronto. Every night we talk on the telephone about many things. Mom always asks why we can't discuss things in person the next day, and I tell her that Lorraine and I are forging our friendship by phone. Sometimes it's easier to tell secrets on the phone than face-to-face. I told Lorraine that I miss sleeping with Treat at night very much, but missing her makes me feel like a big baby. Lorraine told me that she feels like a baby when she has to count on her fingers every single time she does a math problem. She said she always feels like crying during our monthly math tests and cries at home whenever she gets a D or an F. She said she has never ever admitted those things to anyone before. I felt honored to be trusted with her secrets.

I am trying very hard to help Lorraine with her math. I helped her make flashcards so that she could memorize her arithmetic facts. To calm her down during math tests I taught her a relaxation exercise that Mom had taught me from one of her college psychology courses. ("Breathe in peace and calm; breathe out anxiety and fear.") I imagined what Ms. Roseman-Keller would say that would make her feel better.

"You have a talent for words," I told Lorraine. "Maybe you can figure out a way to use your words to help you with numbers."

Meanwhile my vocabulary is improving. Lorraine and I have learned many interesting and unusual words that we are able to bring up in everyday conversations with each other. For example:

1. Certain foods are *repugnant* to me.
2. When I visit a beautiful forest, I think about the *xylems* of all the plants in it.
3. As your *confidante,* I learn how you feel about things.
4. It is very romantic when the moon, the earth, and the sun are in *syzygy.*
5. It's hard to *feign* feeling happy when you really feel sad.

I can tell that other girls in the class wish they were as close to Lorraine as I am. Lorraine is very trendy. Last week she came to school wearing her hair pinned up on one side only. The next day five other girls (including me) did the very same thing.

If I weren't planning to move to Brooklyn in the near future, I would want Lorraine to be my eternal best friend. Once I read in a book about two very good friends who participated in a beautiful friendship ceremony under the drooping leaves of a willow tree. Each girl pricked the middle finger of her right hand with a sterilized pin until a tiny drop of blood came out. Then they touched their fingers together and read the following pledge:

From the deepest part of our souls
We pledge Eternal Friendship
And mingle our ruby-red blood
Forever.

Maybe Lorraine and I could become eternal pen pals, writing letters forever, between L.A. and Brooklyn.

Yesterday, while we were working hard at our homework together in the backyard, I noticed something about Lorraine that made me feel a little bit jealous.

"Lorraine!" I said. "You are starting to get breasts!"

"Yes, I am becoming a woman," she said.

I wonder when I'll get to be a woman. Sometimes I feel like the whole wide world is changing and leaving me behind.

La-La

FARLA: A faraway music. A forest laden
with green. A fair lady (with breasts).

Dear Baby,

D is for DOG and E is for EGG. I say E is for
ECHH!

I am taping a postcard I received from Bubbie
Flo into this book. It is a example of how nice
she is.

Dear Farla,

I miss you, too. We'll have fun when
you visit me.

I understand how you must feel
about Treat, and how much you will
miss snuggling with her at night. But
please don't worry too much; she may
have fun outdoors.

Speaking of cats, I am feeding two
new strays who appeared at my back
door one day last week. One I call Pop,
because he's fat almost to bursting; the
other I call Chase-My-Tail.

Love,
Bubbie Flo

✦✦✦✦✦✦✦✦✦✦ Tuesday, November 21

Dear Baby,

I have changed my name. My new name is Zoë. It means "life," from a Greek word. I think it is a beautiful name. It is pronounced *Zo*-ee. The two little dots over the *e* give it the "ee" sound. I do not need a *dim.* because Zoë already sounds like a nickname. I do not need a *var.* because I like it just the way it is.

It is the Platonic ideal of names. Ms. Roseman-Keller taught us that Plato was a wise Greek philosopher who believed that everything in the real world has its perfect version in the ideal world. I think the name Zoë comes close to perfection.

I told my family and my friends and Ms. Roseman-Keller that from now on I will answer only to the name of Zoë, not Farla.

Zoë

P.S. Lorraine thinks it's a lovely name, too. She wrote me a beautiful poem, and here it is:

POEM TO MY BEST FRIEND
Zoë, you are prettë, fun, and crazë,
And you make me happë.

40

Dear Baby,

I am curled up in my window seat, writing to you. It is early in the morning. I see Treat scampering about the backyard, chasing a black cat. The sunshine is making our lemon tree sparkle, and our poinsettia bush is heavy with dew. I will miss that beautiful view with all my heart, and will hold it inside of me, forever and ever.

I am still the grouchiest person in the house. Mom and Charlie seem very happy all the time. Music is always playing, and Mom dances to it to stay in shape. Charlie smiles a lot and tells jokes. Even when he sneezes, he makes a great big happy deal out of it, like he's singing opera or something. It's hard to describe, sort of like "Ahchoooahee!" He has started building the bookshelves for the spare room downstairs and sings while he works. And, of course, Great-aunt Sally is in love with her vacuum.

The doctor looked at the test results and told Mom and Charlie that you are developing normally so far. The doctor also knows whether you are a girl or a boy, but Mom and Charlie don't want to be told. They said they want to find out your sex during the wonder of the birth process.

41

Everybody had a very hard time remembering to call me Zoë. Mom said, "Oh, dear, do I have to? I miss my Farla!" Charlie kept calling me "Farla, uh, Zoë," and Great-aunt Sally flatout refused to change. She said she was too old to remember something like that, and Farla was a perfectly good name that had served me well enough for almost twelve years. The only two people who always remembered to call me Zoë were Lorraine and Ms. Roseman-Keller.

I decided to help everybody remember my new name. I went to Tommy's Tees and chose a beautiful fuchsia T-shirt. I asked the man at the store to print ZOË on the back with his special machine. He said it would cost two dollars more for the dots, so I put the dots on myself with a felt pen when I got home.

The T-shirt worked. My friends at school remembered my new name all morning. Then Roy walked by my desk to sharpen his precious Not Yours pencil.

"Nice shirt, squirt," he said, patting me on the back as he passed by.

I decided to ignore the insult because if you show people that their teasing bothers you, they will continue to tease you just to get your attention.

"Thank you for the compliment," I said.

But when Roy passed my seat again, he pointed at my back, making grunting noises and scratching himself like a gorilla. The class started to giggle. Roy had taped a big o over the ë of my new name, so it said ZOO instead of ZOË. Lisa, a girl in the class who sits in back of me, pulled the sign off. I was so mad that I called Roy a baby and a creep right to his face.

Lorraine tried to make me feel better. She said, "Zoë, maybe Roy did that because he likes you."

I find that hard to believe. Roy did that because he's immature. After lunch I found a note on my desk that said:

I APPOLIGIZE (sic)

> Your classmate,
> Roy

I put the *sic* there, just now. (When you put *sic* after a word, it means that the spelling mistake was the other person's and not yours.) I crumpled up the note and threw it on the floor. Now I don't even feel like being called Zoë anymore or wearing my fuchsia T-shirt.

Last night I went downstairs to talk to Mom about what had happened in school and my worries about my physical development and other things. Charlie was in the kitchen setting up some special lights. He was getting ready to photograph a trout lying on a plate for your F-is-for-FISH picture. He said, "Oh, hi, Farla, uh, Zoë." I asked him where Mom was, and he said that she had been falling asleep over her books and decided to go to bed early. I was feeling so bad that I even started to tell Charlie about everything, but then I changed my mind because he seemed all wrapped up in your old trout.

So I just poured myself a glass of milk, ate some corn chips, brushed my teeth, and went to bed. I lay there for a long time. When I finally fell asleep, I had a dream about Treat, chasing a gorilla who was wearing a T-shirt.

Farla

✦✦✦✦✦✦✦✦✦✦ Sunday, December 3

Dear Baby,

Here is a story I wrote myself:

A THANKSGIVING TALE

Once upon a time there was a turkey named Tom. He looked at the world with joy in his heart. He loved the shining bright sun, the green, green grass, and the taste of the corn that he ate. But most of all he loved the farmer's son, Lance. Lance kept his trough clean and his water pure and fresh. Lance combed Tom's feathers and fed him sweet apple slices. Lance sang songs to him and Tom gobbled back. They were good friends.

But one day the axman came. The ax glistened like diamonds. Lance cried and begged his father to save Tom's life, but his father stated, "You may cry, but Tom is to be our dinner."

That night, when all were asleep and the moon was high in the sky, Lance crept into Tom's pen and whispered a story in his turkey ear. Tom ruffled his red feathers and said, "Thank you, thank you. Please climb aboard."

The next morning Lance and Tom were gone. The farmer and his wife searched high and low, and the towns-people searched the countryside, too, but to no avail. Lance and Tom were never to return. The farmer and his wife missed their kind son greatly and became vegetarians ever after.

THE END

I felt like crying after I wrote that story. Great-aunt Sally worked hard on her cooking on Thanksgiving Day, but all I could think of was Tom the Turkey. I said that I didn't want any turkey, thank you.

Mom said, "Why, Farla! You've never turned down turkey before. Great-aunt Sally worked very hard on this meal!"

Great-aunt Sally looked hurt. I felt guilty, so I made sure I ate everything else, like stuffing, vegetables, and pumpkin pie, except I couldn't eat the tomato aspic, which kept shivering on my plate.

Then Mom said, "Well, things sure will be different around here next year with a baby in the house."

Hadn't she noticed? I thought. Things were different already! Then Mom and Charlie got that moony look they always get, staring at each other and thinking their ESP thoughts. It always looks like they have ESP powers when they do that, like they know how to read each other's minds or something. Who knows? Maybe love does strange things to something in your brain, so ESP is possible.

It is a new month now, December. Hanukkah is only nineteen days away. Christmas Eve is two days later. We are now an interfaith household.

The Wondrous Story says you are about ten inches long and weigh one pound. You have hair on your head, and fingernails and toenails. Mom feels you moving around more and more.

G is for GIRAFFE and H is for HOUSE. Eighteen more boring pictures to go.

Farla

✦✦✦✦✦✦✦✦✦✦ Monday, December 11

Dear Baby,

Ms. Roseman-Keller is teaching us how to write Japanese haiku poetry. She says haikus usually have five syllables in the first line, seven syllables in the next line, and five syllables in the last. Like this:

December is here
Holiday visits and hugs
From someone you love.

Ms. Roseman-Keller said you can really see and feel things with a short poem like that. She's right. I stare out the window and wait until the right words for my feelings come to me. Here they come:

December feeling
Sad is a gray little cat
With a cold wet nose.

Lorraine says her family has had the same beautiful holiday traditions for years and years. Her mother always bakes cookies shaped like stars and trees and bells. They always gather around the piano on Christmas morning to sing carols. She has had the same Santa Christmas stocking for twelve years.

Since we are now an interfaith household at our house, I don't know what our tradition is.

News of the week: Mom is very busy studying for her final exams, I is for ICE CREAM, J is for JAM, and you have two new sweaters. Only fifteen more days until I go to Bubbie Flo's for winter vacation. She telephoned us from Florida, where she is visiting friends. She can't wait for me to meet her new stray cat named Max.

Farla

Dear Baby,

Lorraine came over after school today. We went up to my room and sat in my window seat together. I poured out the deepest part of my soul to Lorraine. She has nice big listening eyes. I told her how bothered I am about you, unborn baby, and about losing my room, and how I will be moving to Brooklyn in the near future.

"I will miss you a lot," said Lorraine.

"I will miss you, too," I told her. "But my late dad's mother, Bubbie Flo, is a lonely widow with no relatives living nearby. She needs me."

Lorraine said she understood. Then she told me about her cousin Ariana, who has a new baby in her house who cries all night long, so that her cousin Ariana can hardly keep her eyes open the next day in school. At least at Bubbie Flo's I'll be able to get my rest.

Speaking about Lorraine's eyes, she wears Mauve Magic eyeshadow on her eyelids in a very tasteful way. Her sister Cheryl gave it to her. Lorraine put a tiny bit on my eyelids. She said it made me look exotic.

When I went downstairs for dinner, Mom asked, "What's that purple guck on your eyelids?"

I told her it wasn't guck, and that all the other girls were wearing Mauve Magic to enhance their eyelids. (Actually only three other girls.)

Great-aunt Sally put her two cents in. "Children in my day wouldn't even think of wearing face makeup except for Halloween or playacting. Or if they happened to be performing in the circus."

Charlie said my eyes didn't need enhancing and Mom said I looked sick, not exotic, and to wash it off immediately. And if she found me wearing makeup again, she would take away my allowance.

Nobody understands anything around here.

Farla

✦✦✦✦✦✦✦✦✦ Wednesday, December 20

Dear Baby,

It was not a good day today.

Lorraine, Lisa, and I decided to go to the mall after school to do some holiday shopping. On the way there Lorraine started telling us how every year her dad dresses up as St. Nick on Christmas Eve, and they all pretend not to recognize him. Lisa said that every year they have a huge Hanukkah party at her grandparents' house. Her Uncle Ed always hides chocolate pennies for all the kids to find. I was tired of hearing about family traditions.

Then Lorraine and Lisa started discussing the gifts they were hoping to get. Lisa said she wanted a tape of her favorite group, the Mystiques, a ring, and a straight skirt like Ms. Roseman-Keller wears. Lorraine wanted a tape of her favorite group, the Crowd, an unabridged dictionary, and a bra with lace on it. I wondered if anyone in my house had any idea who my favorite group is (Luscious Froods). I was getting grouchier and grouchier.

At the mall Lorraine bought a beautiful Christmas-tree ornament for each one of the members of her family. She said every member of her family does that for every other family member. It is an old, old family tradition.

I bought a bottle of Whiff o' Roses for Mom, a tie for Charlie, and a box of chocolates for Great-aunt Sally. I bought an I Love L.A. T-shirt for Bubbie Flo. I spent all of my money, except for six dollars that Great-aunt Sally had given me to buy her some knitting wool.

Then we looked at makeup. Lovely pink-and-red tubes of lipstick. Creamy lip gloss. Circus-bright circles of eyeshadow in blue, violet, earthy brown, and smoky gray tones. Makeup comes in tones, not colors. We squirted ourselves with free samples of cologne.

Lorraine and Lisa tried on lipstick samples and then bought their own. They asked me why I didn't buy any.

"I'm not sure I like these tones very much," I said.

"I think Pink Thrill would look great with your complexion," Lorraine said. "Try it on."

I picked up the lipstick sample. It smelled sweet and forbidden. I smeared some on my lips.

"Oh, you look so elegant and sophisticated! You look almost sixteen!" said Lisa.

I squinted at myself in a mirror. I looked at Lorraine and Lisa, who I thought looked very sophisticated. Oh, how I wanted to be sophisticated, too!

Then I remembered all the silly sweaters and hats you already had, unborn baby. I gave Great-aunt Sally's knitting money to the salesclerk and bought the Pink Thrill.

When I got home, I snuck into the bathroom and looked at myself in the mirror again. In that mirror I looked the same as I always look—same face, same complexion, but with bigger, pinker lips. I wiped off the lipstick. What would I tell Great-aunt Sally about her money? I wondered.

"What's that sweet smell?" asked Charlie at dinner, sniffing. "A new air freshener?"

"Oh, the house is always full of nice, clean smells since Great-aunt Sally took over," said Mom in a happy voice.

I knew the smell was me and my sample cologne. Soon they would figure out I was hanging around makeup counters. I could feel my left eye starting to twitch.

After dinner Great-aunt Sally said, "Well, as soon as the dishes are done, I'll relax with my knitting. Let me see the wool you bought for me this afternoon, dear."

I gave the money to a hungry hobo. A dog ran away with the wool. I was held up and, fearing for my life, handed over all my money without a fight. Those were the lies that went through my mind. Here is the lie that came out:

"I'm s-sorry, Great-aunt Sally. I put my hand in my pocket and the money was gone. It must have fallen out. I'm very, very sorry, but I promise with all my heart that I will pay you back out of my future allowance earnings."

I stuttered just like that when I told her. It is not easy to lie.

"Oh, dear," said Mom, looking worried. "I hope there isn't a pickpocket at your school."

"If you have a hole in your pocket, let me see it so I can mend it," said Great-aunt Sally.

And that was that. They believed me and trusted me! But I didn't feel relieved, and I didn't feel happy. I suddenly remembered that older retired people have to budget their money a lot.

You are the only one who knows that I am a liar and a thief, unborn baby.

Farla

P.S. I threw the Pink Thrill away.
P.P.S. I leave for Bubbie Flo's in six days.

✝✝✝✝✝✝✝✝✝✝ Tuesday, December 26

Dear Baby,

Hello. Here I am writing to you from the sky! I am now in an airplane flying to New York.

I just ate lunch, and I had crepes for the first time. There is a man on a business trip sitting beside me. He showed me a picture of his daughter, who is my age. Soon I will see a movie.

I have lots of time to daydream on an airplane. I looked out the window and saw a beautiful blanket of clouds underneath me. I imagined what it would feel like to jump on the clouds, or to taste them, or to lie down on a cloud-bed.

By the way, the holidays turned out to be okay, I guess. You will like it when you get older. Great-aunt Sally told the story of Christmas. Mom told the story of Hanukkah. Mom said that both holidays have the symbol of light in them, a star and a flame for hopefulness.

I got my own cologne from Mom and Charlie (Perty Sweet) and a stereo-radio-cassette recorder. Great-aunt Sally gave me a gift certificate from the Rock Shoppe.

Soon I will see my Bubbie Flo. I can't wait.

I have to stop writing because the movie is beginning now.

Farla in the Sky

✦✦✦✦✦ Wednesday, December 27, 1 A.M.

Dear Baby,

Here I am, writing to you from Brooklyn! It's one o'clock in the morning, but I can't sleep because my body says it's really ten P.M. L.A. time. Bubbie Flo is asleep in her room. I sleep on the couch in the living room. Bubbie Flo said I could watch TV as late as I wanted to since I'm on vacation, and she would let me sleep in. On top of the TV is a big blown-up picture of me sitting on my real dad's shoulders. It's the same picture that I have in my bedroom at Mom's house.

Bubbie Flo says that I have a more mature look to my face than when she last saw me. She says that I have my dad's eyes but my mom's smile and chin. And of course, Bubbie Flo's nose.

Bubbie Flo has changed, too. While I've been wishing for more curviness, she has been working hard to get rid of some of hers. She has lost twenty pounds. She also put a reddish tint in her hair to remove the gray. She looks very nice. At first I didn't recognize her. I got off the airplane and I saw a lady with reddish hair waving and smiling at me, and then I got closer and saw that it was my Bubbie Flo. After a while I didn't notice the differences, and she looked like the same grandmother I knew before.

Another change is that Bubbie Flo has a brand-new microwave oven in her kitchen. She says she loves it. She says it saves her a lot of time. Also she can cook one-serving Weight-Be-Gone dinners in it without heating up her entire kitchen. But reheated microwaved potato pancakes don't taste the same as fresh-fried ones. I guess I was disappointed, but of course I didn't say anything, because I'm a guest.

I didn't have a chance to discuss moving to Brooklyn with Bubbie Flo. We mostly talked about what we're going to do while I'm here on vacation. I met Pop and Chase-My-Tail and a smaller cat named Snoop, who reminds me of Treat except Snoop's a tabby. Bubbie Flo laughed when I asked about the new stray cat named Max. She told me that she had said she had a new friend, not a new stray. She met him in Miami.

Mom called tonight. She said the house was so quiet without me, she even misses the Luscious Froods. I didn't know she knew their name.

Farla

✦✦✦✦✦✦✦✦✦ Thursday, December 28

Dear Baby,

I can't write a lot this time because I'm very tired. It's hard work being a tourist!

Today we went into New York City. We took a subway, which is an extremely fast train. In Brooklyn this subway is sometimes called the El because it travels elevated above the streets. When you get to New York City, it goes underground. It is noisy and fun.

When we got off the subway, we walked and walked. People here walk very fast, and everybody wears sneakers so they can walk even faster. There are so many people! And cars and taxis and sirens and buildings. Bubbie Flo bought me a new dress that swirls out like a flower when I dance. In a New York deli I ate a sandwich that was so big I could hardly bite it. I had tea in a fancy hotel, and raspberry mousse for the first time. Then we took a long ride around Central Park in a buggy pulled by a horse.

I am going to write a postcard to Lorraine now. It's nine o'clock in Brooklyn but only six o'clock in L.A.

Farla

✦✦✦✦✦✦✦✦✦✦✦ Friday, December 29

Dear Baby,

Today we went to Radio City Music Hall in Manhattan and saw some famous dancers called the Rockettes and a movie. Then we ate lunch at a restaurant where you can watch people ice-skating when you look out the window.

There's a little bit of snow on the ground. It's cold. I have to wear a hat and coat and a scarf. Mom called again tonight and said it was very warm in Los Angeles—seventy-five degrees! Then she said, "Hear that banging? That's Charlie building your bookshelves." And then Charlie got on to say hello. He said, "K is for Kitten and L is for Lamp."

Farla

✦✦✦✦✦✦✦✦✦✦✦Sunday, December 31

Dear Baby,

Since I last wrote you, I've been to the Statue of Liberty, a play, and a fancy restaurant. I tasted a snail, just a tiny bit of one. I kept thinking

about the snails that make silvery paths on our driveway in L.A.

Farla

✦✦✦✦✦✦✦✦✦✦✦✦ Monday, January 1

Dear Baby,

Happy New Year to you. This is the year you will be born in.

Last night we called Mom and Charlie and Great-aunt Sally to wish them a Happy New Year. Mom told me some news that made me feel bad. She said they found Treat sniffing around a dead mouse in the backyard. I guess Treat became a predator while I was gone.

At midnight we heard fireworks outside. Bubbie Flo and I fed her cat friends a special New Year's dinner of fresh microwaved chicken breast. I wondered if Treat had anything enjoyable to eat besides mouse. L.A. seemed very, very far away. It wasn't even the New Year there yet. I missed Mom very much.

I asked Bubbie Flo if she ever got lonely, like I did. She said yes.

"Do you ever think about my dad?" I asked.

"Always," she said. Her eyes had tears in them.

Then I told Bubbie Flo my worries about you and your blue-eye genes, unborn baby.

"Genes, shmenes," said Bubbie Flo. "I know your daddy would have wanted you and your mom to have a family again. And it will be nice to have a sister or brother, too, no matter what color its eyes."

I told her what it felt like, living with strangers. "I think about moving to Brooklyn and being your family," I said.

Bubbie Flo hugged me hard, and then she told me some surprising news. She said that her friend Max had asked for her hand in marriage, and she was going to move to Florida.

"If you lived with me, you'd still have to get used to a new stepgrandfather," she said, "who smokes cigars. But I'd love for you to come and visit whenever you want."

Well, that's that. Bubbie Flo doesn't need me like she used to, and I sure don't like cigars. So I guess I'll be flying home tomorrow for good. But Charlie and Great-aunt Sally and you, unborn baby, are not my real family, no matter what Bubbie Flo says.

Farla

Dear Baby,

Well, here I am, back in L.A. Things are different, even though I was only gone for a week and a half. I have a new bedroom downstairs, and Charlie has started painting my old room for you. Mom is fatter, and she rests more than she used to. She goes to bed at nine o'clock every night. *The Wondrous Story* says you are about twelve inches long now and weigh one and a half pounds. Your skin is wrinkled and red. Sometimes you cry and suck your thumb. But what do *you* have to cry about?

Last night was my first night in my new bedroom. All my furniture is the same, except that I have more bookshelves now. I hung the picture of me and my dad on the wall beside my bed. I lay there, listening to my new heater humming like a faraway spaceship. I thought that if I stayed very still and concentrated very hard, maybe I could transport myself back to that happy time, back to the very second when Mom snapped the picture.

MOM: Smile, everybody! Say "Cheese"!
DAD: I don't want cheese! How about some
    ice cream?

THREE-YEAR-OLD ME: Yay! Let's go!

But, anyway, it didn't work. I was still downstairs, alone in my new room, with Great-aunt Sally snoring down the hall and Charlie snoring upstairs in bed beside my tired, fat mom, who has wrinkled you inside of her.

I started feeling kind of sorry for myself, and I cried a little into my pillow. I thought about how everybody has somebody. Mom has Charlie, Bubbie Flo has her Max. After a while I got out of bed and snuck outside. I found Treat lying under a lawn chair in the backyard. I picked her up and brought her inside to bed with me. She felt warm and soft, and we both fell asleep right away. Just like old times.

Farla

✚✚✚✚✚✚✚✚✚✚✚✚ Monday, January 8

Dear Baby,
Other things are different, too.
During the winter vacation, when I was visiting Bubbie Flo, Lorraine and Lisa spent a lot of time together, forging their friendship. I guess

Lorraine thought I wasn't returning to Los Angeles. I have a jealous feeling inside of me. I don't like it. It feels like a hard black stone inside my heart. Lorraine asked me if I minded if Lisa joined in our dictionary conversations. She said Lisa felt left out when we used big words that we both understood but she didn't. I said I thought it would be too *cumbersome* (a word from last week) to include her. Lorraine said I didn't have to sound so grumpy and that it wasn't very kind to leave her out.

I think Lisa is too boy-crazy. All she wants to talk about is her next-door neighbor, Rick, who goes to junior high. I don't think you need extra vocabulary words to talk about the same old topic day in and day out.

Another difference is Mr. Gilmore. Ms. Roseman-Keller is such a wonderful and experienced teacher that she helps other people learn how to be good teachers, too. Mr. Gilmore is a student teacher in our classroom. He seems very nervous. He looks at his notes too much and clears his throat a lot and sometimes forgets our names. Today he called me Marla.

Mr. Gilmore is teaching us about a man named Pericles. He was a leader in ancient Greece who believed in giving citizens equality and freedom of speech and good jobs. He gave humane treatment to resident aliens and slaves. Because people were happy and proud of their state, they built beautiful buildings and wrote creative plays and discussed important ideas in philosophy. Mr. Gilmore assigned us a class project on civic responsibility. Just like a good citizen during Pericles' time, each of us is to think of an activity that is creative and helpful and that also enhances our own self-esteem. I had a few good ideas:

1. Bake good, nourishing loaves of bread and distribute them to the poor and homeless.
2. Organize a big Children's Talent Show and write to somebody famous to be the master of ceremonies. Donate the proceeds to cancer research.

I discussed my ideas with Ms. Roseman-Keller and Mr. Gilmore. They said they were kind and thoughtful, but a little too ambitious. They suggested I think of something on a smaller scale. Mom said, "What about baby-sitting?" She had seen an ad in the newspaper for a seminar for boys and girls to teach them how to be Super Sitters. I told her that wasn't creative enough.

Farla

P.S. I forgot to tell you that I am paying Great-aunt Sally back. I give her two dollars a week out of my three-dollar-a-week allowance.

✝✝✝✝✝✝✝✝✝✝✝ Tuesday, January 16

Dear Baby,

Yesterday Lorraine and Lisa and I were walking home from school. Lisa said that the air was redolent with the smell of freshly cut grass, and I pretended that I didn't hear her. I figured that *redolent* was probably her word for the day, that she was trying to join our dictionary conversations. We were passing by the Haunted House. A car drove up to it, and a man and a lady got out. The lady was wearing a jacket that people who sell houses sometimes wear. There was still a FOR SALE sign on the front lawn.

"They're never going to sell it," I said.

"Farla thinks that house is haunted," said Lorraine. "She even thinks a ghost swims in the swimming pool!"

Lisa snorted. "Oh, Farla," she said, "do you still believe that?"

"Farla has a vivid imagination!" said Lorraine.

"I used to think a ghost lived there a long time ago, when I was just a baby!" said Lisa. Then Lorraine and Lisa giggled and made ghost noises.

I felt the hard black jealous stone inside my heart and that gurgly lump in my throat. All of a sudden some words popped out of my mouth before I had a chance to think.

"I'm not a baby!" I shouted. "But I know someone who still needs to count on her fingers like a baby when she does her math problems! And she cries like a baby after every single math test!"

Lorraine turned very red. I wished I could grab my words in midair and swallow them back inside of me again.

"I didn't call you a baby," she said in a soft, cold voice. "But I know someone who still needs to sleep with kitty cats."

And then she walked up her front walk without saying good-bye. Today we didn't speak to each other all day in school.

Farla

Dear Baby,

Lorraine and I are still not on speaking terms. She spends lots of time with Lisa. They both have T-shirts with a fancy l on the back. I heard them saying they are both going to volunteer their services in Lisa's father's office for their civic-responsibility project. He is a veterinarian.

I wish I hadn't given away Lorraine's secret. It hurts so much not to have a best friend anymore. What's the use of a big room for sleepovers if you haven't got a good friend to sleep over?

Today when Mr. Gilmore was teaching us, the map of ancient Greece kept rolling up and the chalk squeaked. Everytime that happened, the class laughed and groaned. I feel sorry for him. I think he's understanding. I told him that I was having a bit of trouble thinking of a good idea for my project, and he said that I shouldn't worry, that an idea will come to me. While I was in the shower this morning I thought I had my idea: organizing a computer service to match up stray puppies and kittens with sad or lonely people. But by the time I dried myself off, I realized that idea was too ambitious, too.

Farla

P.S. Even Treat has someone special—a big black cat who yowls for her outside my bedroom window every night.

M is for mustache, N is for NOSE, and O is for OWL (from the L.A. Zoo).

✦✦✦✦✦✦✦✦✦✦✦ Saturday, January 20

Dear Baby,

I am so worried.

Mom is in the hospital. She felt some pains today, and Charlie had to drive her there right away. Everybody is afraid that you are going to be born too early, before you are ready. *The Wondrous Story* says babies need to grow inside their mothers for nine months, but you've been growing for only seven.

At suppertime Charlie came home from the hospital alone. He looked tired. "Your mom has to stay in the hospital overnight for observation, but I think everything is going to be okay," he said.

Then Charlie, Great-aunt Sally, and I went out for pizza. Charlie ordered it with extra cheese and pepperoni, just the way I like it. But I wasn't really very hungry.

Mom just called to say good-night, so I feel a little better.

How are you feeling, unborn baby? Are you hurting? Are you very lonely and afraid?

Your half sister,
Farla

✦✦✦✦✦✦✦✦✦✦✦✦ Friday, January 26

Dear Baby,

Hello, hello! Mom is home and both of you are fine, but Mom has to rest all the time. She lies in her big bed all day long and reads and watches TV. She gets up only to eat meals or shower or go to the bathroom.

When I come home from school at three o'clock, I lie on Mom's bed and the two of us watch "As My Children Grow" on TV. Everybody's life on that show is very complicated. There are lots of murders and love affairs and financial failures and stress. Compared to "As My Children Grow," my life is pretty predictable. Every morning Charlie drives me to school. I see the same kids and teachers day after day. I come home, watch "As My Children Grow" with Mom, do some homework, eat dinner, do some more homework, watch some TV or read a book. Some nights I write to you. But just because my life is predictable doesn't mean it doesn't have stress. Lorraine and I are still not talking to each other. I stare at the telephone and wish that Lorraine and I could have long conversations like we used to.

Mom says when you have a hurt inside, it helps to share it with another person. Two people sharing one person's hurt divides it up and makes you feel better, she says. I wish I could tell Mom about my fight with Lorraine, or the big lie I told about Great-aunt Sally's money, or all my worries about my physical development and our new family. But if I did that, it would only upset her and cause stress.

Farla

Dear Baby,

Last night I woke up suddenly. It was pitch-black in my room, but I could tell that something was different. I reached over to the side of my bed to hug Treat. She wasn't there. She wasn't at the end of my bed, either.

I could hear a faint rustling noise. I got out of bed and tiptoed out of my room, squinting in the dark. The rustling noise got louder. It seemed to be coming from the room where Great-aunt Sally sleeps. I stopped outside her door, which was half-open. Her night-light was on, and when I looked in, I saw a very strange sight.

A very hairy black and gray creature was scampering around the room. Great-aunt Sally was scampering after it in her nightgown, holding a big book in her hands, ready to strike. The hairy creature had a long, fluffy gray tail. I recognized the tail.

"Wait! Don't hurt her!" I whispered loudly. "It's only Treat!"

You know that bun of hair that Great-aunt Sally pins on during the day and takes off at night? Well, Treat had been snooping around and probably thought the hair was a playmate,

like the black cat she plays with in the backyard. The hair flopped over her eyes. She pulled at it with her claws and was just starting to chew it when I grabbed it and picked her up.

Great-aunt Sally walked slowly over to her bed. She sat down, reached for her glasses on her night table, and put them on. Then she started making these wheezing noises and shaking. I was afraid Great-aunt Sally was having a heart attack.

"Oh, dear!" she said, wheezing.

"Do you want a glass of water?" I asked.

"Oh, dear!" said Great-aunt Sally again. She had tears running down her cheeks. She took off her glasses to wipe her eyes.

"This is very humorous!" she finally said. "Now, tell me how that cat got inside."

I was so relieved that Great-aunt Sally was laughing and not having a heart attack that I told her how lonely I felt at night in my big new room, and how I'd been sneaking outside to bring Treat into my bed, and letting her outside again early in the morning.

I was holding Treat with one hand and Great-aunt Sally's hair knot with the other. "I'm so sorry about your hair," I said. "I promise to pay for any repairs out of my allowance. But please don't tell Mom, Great-aunt Sally. It will upset her."

"My hair knot doesn't look too bad," she said. "But you are offering to pay for a lot of things out of your allowance these days. You must be running low on cash by now," she said.

Suddenly I felt ashamed. "Great-aunt Sally, I have a big confession to make." And then I told her the story of the Pink Thrill and what really happened to her knitting money.

"Oh, Farla, I am so glad you are finally telling the truth," she said. "I know you're having a hard time lately, what with all the changes occurring in your life. But that's no excuse for what you did."

"I know, Great-aunt Sally. But I just wanted to be more grown up, like my friends," I said.

Great-aunt Sally looked stern, but kind. "There are two parts to growing up, young lady," she said. "Growing up on the inside and growing up on the outside. And the first part is more important."

"But how do you do it?" I asked.

"You've already started," she said. "And you can help me more around the house to pay off your debt. Now, put that cat where she wants to be and go back to bed."

So I put Treat outside and fell asleep right away.

Farla

✦✦✦✦✦✦✦✦✦✦✦ Thursday, February 1

Dear Baby,

I have been appointed Head Vacuumer of the house. I have already learned how to make a salad and roast a chicken and bake a tuna casserole. Great-aunt Sally is also teaching me how to knit, but I'm not very good. I keep dropping stitches and having to start the row over. It'll probably end up being a scarf because I can only knit straight down. Great-aunt Sally says it takes great maturity to admit your shortcomings. *Mature Admission:* I'm not a good knitter. All I seem to be doing is dropping stitches. She also says that perseverance is part of maturity and that I should just carry on and something will come of it. So I am.

Farla

P.S. P is for POPCORN.

✦✦✦✦✦✦✦✦✦✦✦ Friday, February 2

Dear Baby,
Some of the girls in my class asked Ms. Rose-

man-Keller if we could have a Valentine's Day party for the sixth grade in the gymnasium, and she said yes. Lorraine and Lisa will be baking Valentine cookies together for the party. They practice dance steps at recess. I'm bringing the paper cups. Some girls say they will be wearing hip-hugging straight skirts to the party, the kind that Ms. Roseman-Keller wears. I can't wear a straight skirt because I don't have hips to hug. I tried one on in Susie's Fashion Mart, and I looked like a human pencil.

I have decided to attend the Super Sitter Training Seminar as my class project. Knowing how to be a Super Sitter will be helpful, even if it's not creative. The seminar is going to be televised on "L.A. Kids," and being on television will probably enhance my self-esteem.

You are now about fifteen inches long and weigh two and a half pounds. Charlie says that unborn babies can hear things. That's a big surprise to me. He says it is quite noisy in the mother's uterus. You can hear Mom talking and her heart beating and the sounds of her eating and drinking. You can hear the TV and the stereo and the sounds of traffic. Can you hear my voice, too?

Farla

P.S. Q is postponed. Charlie wants to think about it. R is for ROSE.

✦✦✦✦✦✦✦✦✦✦✦✦ Monday, February 5

Dear Baby,

I went to the Super Sitter Training Seminar this weekend. There were a lot of girls signed up, including one whole Girl Scout troop. There were only two boys. One boy's name was Darren. I'd never met him before. The other boy was—guess who? Roy. Funny, I never would have thought of him as the baby-sitter type.

A nurse named Sandi was our instructor. She used a doll to teach us many things, like how to perform first aid on cuts and burns, and how to feed, burp, and diaper babies. We learned about emergency phone numbers and how to keep dangerous things such as medicine and household cleaners out of the reach of little kids. We learned which toys are the safest and how to make a Sitter's Surprise Bag. That's a bag that the sitter brings from home filled with things to entertain children.

The TV filming was the most exciting part

of the seminar. Three people entered the room while Sandi the nurse was talking. She stopped to let them introduce themselves. A lady named Tamara was the director. Her job was to tell everybody what to do. A man with a beard named Garth carried a video camera. Another lady named Pam carried a clipboard and took notes.

The cameraman filmed kids giving each other CPR, putting gauze bandages on each other, and being interviewed about why they wanted to be baby-sitters and why they were attending the seminar:

GIRL SCOUT: I would like to earn my own money.
DARREN: I baby-sit for my younger brother a lot, and I want to make sure I know what to do in an emergency.
ANOTHER GIRL: I'm planning to become a pediatrician like my mother and would like some experience with small children before I enter medical school in ten years or so.

Then Tamara, the director, said, "I'll need three kids to demonstrate diapering to our viewers."

Three girls were picked. And guess who was one of them? Yours truly!

"Let's add a boy to that shot!" said the director.

And so Roy was chosen as a fourth "volunteer." He had probably never even touched a diaper before, and Sandi, the nurse, had to show him how to do it. I think I did a pretty good job diapering because I used to have a Wendy Wets doll, and Mom had bought me my own box of paper diapers, so I know the basics.

It was funny when the director kept wanting to shoot the diapering from different angles, and we had to repeat the scene and pretend it was happening for the first time. I learned a lot about TV as well as baby-sitting.

Farla, TV Star

P.S. Here is a letter from Bubbie Flo.

Dear Farla,

I miss you, too. Yes, many cats like to be out at night, and Treat is no exception.

The next time you visit me will be in Florida. Wait until you see the Epcot

Center, the Kennedy Space Center, and
the Everglades!

Enclosed is my recipe for potato
latkes that you asked for. Enjoy! Enjoy!
Tell Sally that shortening gives a very
crispy pancake.

Love,
Bubbie Flo

✝✝✝✝✝✝✝✝✝✝✝Thursday, February 8

Dear Baby,

Today in school Roy announced that he
would be appearing on television tomorrow
night. He explained about the Super Sitter Training Seminar.

Ms. Roseman-Keller smiled at him and said,
"What an informative experience that must have
been!"

But then Roy said, "Don't forget that Farla
was there, too." I was truly surprised that he
was willing to share the spotlight with me.

"We will both be featured demonstrating a
special skill," I said.

Mr. Gilmore wrote on the chalkboard:

Watch Farla and Roy on "L.A. Kids,"
Feb. 9, 6:00 P.M.,
Channel 3.

I hope Lorraine will watch me.

Farla

✦✦✦✦✦✦✦✦✦✦✦✦ Friday, February 9

Dear Baby,
Tonight Charlie, Great-aunt Sally, Mom, and I watched "L.A. Kids" in Mom and Charlie's bedroom. The VCR was set to tape the show, and the telephone-answering machine was on so we wouldn't be disturbed. I imagined all the kids in my class in front of their TV sets, as well as Ms. Roseman-Keller and her husband, Mr. Keller. I wanted Lorraine to wish she were still best friends with a person in the media.

The first part of the program was about talented kids who go to a special high school where they do regular schoolwork but also sing and dance and act in plays. Another part of the show featured what kids in Los Angeles like to eat most for school lunches (peanut butter sandwiches). Then came a commercial. And then another commercial. At last "L.A. Kids" came back on. There was Sandi, the nurse, explaining things. There was Darren, saying that he wanted to know what to do in an emergency. There was a Girl Scout putting a gauze bandage on another Girl Scout. I explained to everybody how the director kept telling her to repeat it over again so they could get the best shot.

"TV changes reality and makes it watchable," said Mom.

I hardly had a chance to think about what Mom had said because all of a sudden there was *this:*

1. A full clear shot of a Girl Scout expertly folding a diaper.
2. A full clear shot of Roy fumbling away with his.
3. Half of the third volunteer.
4. *My right arm.*

You couldn't see how neatly I tucked in the sides like Mom had taught me when I got my Wendy Wets doll. You couldn't see the nurse showing Roy how to do it, or hear him saying,

"Hope the kid won't squirt me!" It seemed like I wasn't even at the Super Sitter Training Seminar.

Even though Great-aunt Sally said, "It's real life that counts, my dear," and Mom said she knew I was a terrific diaper changer, and Charlie didn't say much but tried to make me laugh during dinner ("Did you hear the story about the nearsighted turtle that fell in love with an army helmet?"), I still felt bad. I know it sounds silly, but I guess I want to know what it feels like to be featured.

Farla

✦✦✦✦✦✦✦✦✦ Wednesday, February 14

Dear Baby,

Today was the Valentine's Day party at school. I almost decided to feign an illness and not go because I don't know how to dance. But Mom is very strict about staying home from school without a good reason. And she is an expert at spotting illness faking, and I can never fool her.

So I put on my new blue dress that Bubbie Flo bought me, the one that swirls out like a flower when I twirl around. I took a book to read and my paper cups. Charlie and Great-aunt Sally were at the breakfast table. Mom was still asleep upstairs.

Mom had never forgotten about Valentine's Day before. I remembered a tradition that Mom and I used to have, back in the days when she was a single parent to me. I would go to a flower shop and so would she, and we would buy each other a single red rose. Then we would go to a restaurant for dinner. Once a man played his violin near our table the whole time we were eating.

"All dressed up!" said Charlie. "What's the occasion?"

"We're having a party at school for Valentine's Day," I said.

"Oh?" said Great-aunt Sally. "Is it February the fourteenth already?"

Charlie drove me to school, and just before I got out of the car, he said, "Farla, listen." I thought he was going to tell me another joke. But then he said, "Everybody feels nervous at times. Some people just hide it better."

At school we did regular work in the morning. But at lunchtime all the sixth-graders went to the gymnasium, which didn't look like the gymnasium at all. The Decorations Committee had put red and white streamers on the walls, and dangling from the basketball nets were red and white balloons. Taped music was playing loudly. The Refreshments Committee had brought taco chips and potato chips and corn chips and plenty of sodas to drink. Some kids had made ham and cheese sandwiches and peanut butter and jelly sandwiches. I put my paper cups on the table.

Ms. Roseman-Keller was wearing a red and white dress, and Mr. Gilmore had a red carnation in his lapel. I counted fifteen girls who had straight skirts on, including Lorraine and Lisa. Lorraine's shoes were the kind that had laces around the ankles, and they were red, too.

If everybody felt nervous, they were sure hiding it well, I thought. I sat on a chair tapping my foot, pretending to be listening to the music. After a while I got up, carrying my book, and went to the girls' bathroom. I sat in a bathroom stall for a long time, feeling so alone. Soon somebody else came into the bathroom and went into the stall next to mine. The music continued to play loudly in the gymnasium. I imagined how much fun everybody was having, dancing.

The shoes in the next-door stall made a shuffling noise, and then I noticed what they looked like. They were bright red with red laces around that person's ankles.

"Farla?" asked the red shoes.

"Lorraine?" I answered.

"Look at this," she said. Her hand reached into my stall, holding an envelope. Inside the envelope I found a Valentine card that said To FARLA, A TRUE FRIEND, and inside the Valentine was a February math test with a big red A on it.

"I studied my flashcards," said Lorraine. "And I used my words, just like you suggested. All through the test I told myself that the fractious fractions were felicitous, and the devilish decimals were really demure, and the pusillanimous percentages were really as pliable as they could be. Soon I wasn't afraid of them anymore. I breathed in lots of peace and calm and breathed out all my anxiety and fear. And it worked. I have you to thank."

"Oh, Lorraine," I said. "I'm sorry I gave away your secret. I was just jealous because you and Lisa are growing up faster than I am."

"And I'm sorry I made fun of you sleeping with Treat."

Lorraine–in–the–bathroom–stall was quiet for a few seconds. "I have a confession to make," she said. "I had no right to make fun of you, because *I* still play with dolls—I pretend that I'm an older sister. I'm jealous of you because you're going to be one. I will always, always be the baby in my family, and you will always, always be the oldest like my sister Cheryl."

That was something I had never thought of before. Lorraine was jealous of me because of you, unborn baby, and I would be an older sister forever.

Then I had an idea. "Well," I said, "if there's such a thing as a godmother and a godfather, why couldn't you be a godsister for this baby? Then you could be an older sister, too."

"I would like that," said Lorraine.

We could still hear the music coming from the gymnasium. But when we went back to the party, I was surprised to see that nobody was dancing. All of the boys were hanging around the food, pretending that the main reason they were at the party was to eat. Some of the boys were laughing very loudly and floating chips in their sodas. Two boys had a burping contest until Mr. Gilmore told them to stop. Most of the girls were sitting in groups around the room, pretending that the reason they were there was to talk to their friends. Some of them began to dance with each other. Lorraine and Lisa taught me some dance steps.

Roy was in charge of the music. His job was to put tapes in a big tape recorder. I went up to him and I said, "Let's let bygones be bygones, okay?" I've always wanted to say that to someone. And he said, "Great!" Maybe next time I'll dance with him.

Lorraine and I walked home together after the party. There was a SOLD sign nailed on top of the FOR SALE sign in front of the Haunted House.

"I hope they like ghosts," I said, and we both laughed.

Then Lorraine told me the real reason she hadn't wanted to dress up for Halloween last October: Her big sisters, Cheryl and Marlene, had laughed at her when she put on her costume. I told her we would dress up as ghosts again next year and take you along, unborn baby, as a baby spook.

When I got home, the house smelled different.

"Great-aunt Sally has a surprise for you," said Mom.

There they were, piled high on a plate, *latkes,* crisp and delicious. Bubbie Flo's recipe, but not like any potato pancakes ever made.

"No mean trick," said Great-aunt Sally, smiling. She looked pretty. Her face was flushed pink from the frying.

The potato pancakes were shaped like hearts!

Farla

✝✝✝✝✝✝✝✝✝✝✝✝ Monday, March 5

Dear Baby,

I was lying on Mom's bed listening to Mozart and reading *The Wondrous Story*. I had my head on Mom's lap, which isn't really a lap anymore. The book says you are now over sixteen inches long and weigh about four pounds. Your eyes are open. Sometimes you swallow some of the water you are floating in and get the hiccups.

"Mom, when will I be a woman?" I asked.

"Soon," she said in a drowsy voice. "Your bell hasn't rung yet. And when it does, it will be beautiful music, like Mozart." That felt like a promise.

The music made me feel warm and shivery at the same time, and the little hairs on my arms stood up on end. I felt you moving inside of her. Maybe you were listening, too.

"Will we have time to do this when the baby

comes, just lie around and listen to music and be with each other?" I asked.

"We'll make time," answered Mom, stroking my hair.

Then I asked her to tell me again the story of the day I was born, and she did. Here it is:

MY TRUE STORY
My parents were on vacation, waiting for me to arrive. It was May twenty-second, and the air smelled like roses. My father was sitting in a chair in the backyard, smoking his pipe. He was reading a novel. He had been wearing a red shirt, but he had taken it off to feel the sun.

My mother was in the house, painting a rocking chair yellow. She felt me moving inside of her. This time it felt different. Each time I moved, she looked at her watch. Soon the times in between the movements got shorter and shorter, and she knew I would soon be born.

So she went out to the backyard, where my father was sitting, and said, "It's time to go to the hospital, Sam."

My father put down his book and his pipe and got up from his chair. My mother went to get the suitcase that had been packed ahead of time, weeks before. She still had yellow paint on her hands, and my father told her later that she had a spot of yellow paint on her nose the whole time. When they got into the car, my mother said, "Maybe you should put on a shirt." My father got out of the car and ran to the backyard and got his red shirt and a rose for Mom.

They drove down Elmby Avenue and waved to Mr. Finch, who was watering his lawn. They turned onto the freeway. The traffic was smooth, and they drove four more miles.

Suddenly the traffic got slower and slower.

"What's happening?" asked my father.

"Was there an accident?" asked my mother.

The traffic crawled along for a long while, and of course they were very worried.

Then they saw the oranges. Thousands and thousands of oranges. Oranges everywhere, spilling onto the freeway

from an overturned truck. Oranges rolling and bouncing onto the divider and
the embankment, orange juice from the
squashed ones wetting the road.

They saw the driver standing unhurt
by the side of his big overturned truck.
A policeman stood beside him, writing
down what had happened. Another policeman waved the cars on.

"We have a baby about to be born!"
shouted my father to the policeman, who
went to the police car and talked into
his radio.

My father turned the car off the freeway. Another police car met our car a
few blocks down and escorted my father
and mother to the hospital, sirens scream-
ing. My mother said I had a triumphant
entrance.

I had heard that part of the story before, but
this time my mother told me something new:

I was born at two o'clock in the afternoon. My parents kissed me hello, and
a nurse cleaned me up and wrapped me
in a pink blanket. Then my father went

97

to call Bubbie Flo on the telephone. "We have a little Sunkist," he told her.

My mother said I grew to be a baby who was plump and sweet, like an orange. My father often called me Sunkist. But when I started preschool, I wanted him to call me by my big-girl name all the time. He always called me Farla after that.

And so I have a nickname, after all. Sunkist. Sun-kissed. Sunny. Sunni. But I don't think I'll change my name again so soon. It's just nice to know the nickname's there.

Farla

✦✦✦✦✦✦✦✦✦✦✦✦✦ Friday, March 23

Dear Baby,
    s is for SANDWICH
    T is for TRUCK
    U is for UMBRELLA
    V is for VASE
    W is for WINDOW
    X is for X (it marks the spot)
    Y is for YARD (ours)
    Z is for ZEBRA (from the L.A. Zoo)
    Q is for QUARTER

I haven't written for a while because I've been very busy. I got an A on my civic-responsibility project. I wrote down everything I had learned at the Super Sitter Training Seminar and presented the information in a speech to my class. I showed them my Sitter's Surprise Bag. I used to keep my socks in it, but now it holds puppets and crayons and paper and Hot Wheels and anything else I want to put in. Mr. Gilmore and Ms. Roseman-Keller said it was very creative. I said I had a responsibility to society to be the best baby-sitter I could possibly be.

I've also been helping out with your room. After Charlie painted the walls, Great-aunt Sally and I helped him put up wallpaper on one side of the room. It's green and white and has bears on it. You have a stuffed blue elephant and a stuffed pink pig sitting in your window seat, which is covered with pillows that Great-aunt Sally made. This afternoon Charlie and I finished painting your crib white. It used to be mine, and a long time ago it was yellow. You have a little white chest of drawers that matches the crib. Some of your clothes are already in it: teeny-tiny nightgowns, teeny-tiny shirts, and teeny-tiny sweaters and hats. There is a rocking chair in a corner of the room. It used to be mine, too.

Your alphabet pictures are hanging up. At first Q was going to be for QUAIL, but Charlie

99

couldn't find one. Then he thought that Q should be for QUEEN, but of course he couldn't find a queen, either. So the other night he set up his special lights and sat me down in a tall chair with a cardboard crown on my head. When the picture was developed, we both examined it together.

"The crown is lopsided," said Charlie.

"I don't look like a queen," I said. "I look like a kid with a piece of cardboard on her head."

Then Charlie said, "I think I'll make it Q is for Quarter, even though your sister or brother will probably think Q is for Money, or Q is for Nickel, and be thoroughly confused. It will be up to us to set the kid straight." Then Charlie looked at me and said, "I don't like F is for Fish, either. I think it will be just as confusing. The kid will probably think F is for Trout, or F is for Dinner."

I laughed. "I think F is for Fish is fine," I said. I was getting to really like that trout with its sparkling popped-out eyes.

Then Charlie went to the baby's closet and pulled out another picture, framed in fuchsia. "I think F is for Farla," he said.

There I was, sitting in the window seat when your room used to be mine. I loved that picture right away. My chin looked just like Mom's.

"I still think F should be for Fish," I said.

Charlie looked disappointed. Then I said, "I want this for my own room, Charlie. Thank you."

Charlie's okay, little baby. Even his jokes are funnier. Maybe he doesn't need to read his step-parenting books so much anymore. Maybe I should have been as nice to him while he was in training as I've been to Mr. Gilmore. Maybe growing up inside means you make more room in your heart.

Farla

SAMPLE JOKE:

CUSTOMER: How much is that bird?

CLERK: Ten dollars, sir.

CUSTOMER: I'll take it. Will you send me the bill?

CLERK: Sorry, sir, you'll have to take the whole bird.

✦✦✦✦✦✦✦✦✦✦✦✦✦ Monday, April 2

Dear Baby,

It is *three o'clock in the morning*! Mom and Charlie woke me up to tell me they were leaving for the hospital. You are on your way! Great-aunt Sally just came into my bedroom to tell me to go back to sleep, because it will be an exciting day.

Welcome, welcome! I will write to you later.

Love,
Farla

✦✦✦✦✦✦✦Monday, April 2 (your birthday)

Dear Annabelle Rose, at last,
(*Vars.*: Anne, Anna; *dims.*: Annie, Rosie, etc.)

Hello, hello! You are a dear baby girl! You weigh six pounds, eight ounces, and are nineteen inches long. You have black hair sticking up in surprised spikes. Your dark blue eyes look kind of surprised, too, as if you weren't expecting the world to look like this! You have soft, silky pink skin that smells sweet, and you know how to yawn and sneeze and suck without ever being taught. You have Charlie's eyes and nose and Mom's and my chin and are like the common denominator of all of us.

I just came home from seeing you in the hospital. We will be bringing you home tomorrow. The first time I saw you, Mom asked, "So what do you think, big sister?" What I thought was, it will take you ten or fifteen years to grow into the scarf I've been knitting for you. So I've decided that the scarf will be a wall hanging for your room, where I will pin pictures and stories and poems that I will make for you.

I have been thinking about what it means to be an older sibling. I can hug you when you're scared, or sad, or lonely. I can teach you things. I will teach you how to tell your right from your left. I will show you how to tie your shoes. I will teach you how to sing a song. I will show you how to eat spaghetti without getting tied up in knots. And when you have a test at school, I will give you some good tips. For instance, when you study your spelling words, you don't just ask someone to test you on them. If you look at the word and spell it out loud, then write it down, then listen to yourself spell it without looking, maybe walk around while doing that, you will have a good chance to get an A. Mom always says, "Use your senses, Farla. Use as many as you can to help you learn!" I will also teach you the dictionary technique that Lorraine taught me and some relaxation exercises. Of course, you won't be worrying about spelling and school for a while, but having an older sibling around will be a good thing even when you are just learning the basics, like how to walk and talk and go to the bathroom at the right time and place.

And I will tell you all about our family traditions, like heart-shaped potato pancakes on Valentine's Day. I'm going to ask Charlie to take a picture of all of us together—me, you, Charlie, Mom, Great-aunt Sally, and Treat. Then I will hang the fish picture in my room and hang up F is for FAMILY in its place. Because now I know what a real family is. Family is a feeling that takes time to grow inside of you.

I wonder if the wise philosophers knew that.

> Love,
> Your big sister,
> Farla